Kevin Brown
KEVIN WITH A "K"

by
Sarah Edwards

SPORTS PUBLISHING INC.
www.SportsPublishingInc.com

©1999 Sports Publishing Inc.
All rights reserved.

Book design, editor: Susan M. McKinney
Cover design: Scot Muncaster
Photos: *The Associated Press,* Georgia Tech, and Wilkinson County Middle
School

ISBN: 1-58261-050-9
Library of Congress Catalog Card Number: 99-61945

SPORTS PUBLISHING INC.
SportsPublishingInc.com

Printed in the United States.

CONTENTS

Kevin grew up in the small town of McIntyre, Georgia.
(AP/Wide World Photos)

Making a Decision

The year was 1987, long before Kevin Brown led the Florida Marlins and then the San Diego Padres to the World Series in consecutive seasons.

It also was long before he became baseball's first $100 million man.

In 1987, the hard-throwing right-hander was still trying to reach the major leagues for good, let alone become a star. Once again he was beginning to see that playing professional baseball at that level was a dream that, for him, might always remain just that—a dream.

The year before, Kevin had moved up to the majors after only two starts in the minors. He had won his big league debut for the Texas Rangers, joining Bobby Witt and Jim Abbott as the only other pitchers in the 1980s who could make that claim. The future seemed so bright, but now, in 1987, his career appeared to be falling apart before it really began.

Kevin spent the 1987 season working his way through the Rangers' minor league system—Single-A Port Charlotte, Florida, to Double-A Tulsa, Oklahoma, to Triple-A Oklahoma City, Oklahoma. He was moving up. That's what those in the Rangers' front office kept reminding him. But Kevin has never been one to humor himself or make-believe that things were any different than what they really are.

The bottom line was that he had won only one game the entire 1987 season. He had gone 1-11,

In 1998, Brown set the Padres' new single-season strikeout record with 257 Ks. (AP/Wide World Photos)

losing his final 11 decisions. His ERA was 6.49.

This wasn't any way to reach the majors, much less stay if he ever got there again. At the end of the season, heading home to Georgia, Kevin decided that he had to change his approach. He knew that the Rangers' coaches were only trying to help him, but too many of them were changing his delivery; they were always reminding him about his pitching mechanics. It had gotten to the point that he was thinking too much, instead of trying to simply to get the batter out.

Nobody is tougher on himself than Kevin Brown. He takes pride in calling himself "the ultimate perfectionist."

Driving home after that season, Kevin decided that he would listen to anybody who tried to help, but he would be the one to decide what to do out on the mound, in the middle of a game.

That "was the beginning," Kevin later said. "I had to get back to thinking it out for myself. There were some hard years to come, but that's the way I've always done it. Since I was young, I've had the good sense to know what to do when I pitch."

Kevin in 1998 World Series action against the Yankees.
(AP/Wide World Photos)

CHAPTER ONE

Growing Up

To fully understand James Kevin Brown, you have to travel to Route 80 east out of Macon toward McIntyre, Georgia.

For a long while you will see nothing but forests of scotch pines and the occasional car passing in the opposite direction. Above the treetops, white towers appear. For those who are continuing through, bound for Wrightsville or Swainsboro, Norristown or Statesboro, these towers, the main plant of the Engelhard Corporation, remain a momentary curiosity. But for us, that's where the story begins.

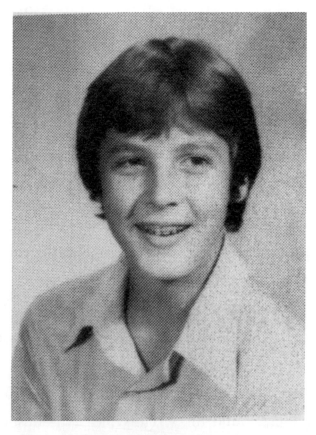

Kevin in the ninth grade.
(Wilkinson County Middle School)

About 11,000 people live in Wilkinson County. More than 1,000 work for Engelhard. Kevin's father worked for Engelhard for 45 years, his uncle for 40 years, his sister is still there and Kevin would be there today if baseball hadn't come along at the 11th hour.

Engelhard mines kaolin, or chalk, used in paints, paper and some medicines. Just below the reddish topsoil in central Georgia lies one of richest reserves in the world. Engelhard and a few smaller companies have been mining this region for 75 years and the vein shows no sign of giving out. Pipelines connect the various quarries with the white-towered plants.

There, amid clouds of steam, the chalk is refined down to vats of slurry that is loaded into railroad tanker cars or container trucks. Once a day, usually early in the afternoon, a Norfolk Southern train bound for Savannah and the sea pulls out of town, pulling that day's load to market.

"Around here basically we're all just country hicks," Kevin's father, Gerald, once said, explaining the region where the family came from. "We don't like to brag or talk real big about ourselves."

Down near the tracks is where Kevin learned to play baseball. Wilkinson County has no recreational department, so the ballfields are mostly supported with Engelhard money and volunteer help.

Back when Kevin was playing, the outfield fence consisted of chicken wire, or hog wire as the local residents call it. Those who coached him or cheered him since he was a boy remember Kevin as a skinny kid, the youngest of Gerald and Carolyn Brown's three children. He was competitive, always one of the best athletes in his age group, but, oddly, never considered the best athlete in any given year.

Kevin's father had only a seventh-grade education. When he started working for the company, he made 60 cents an hour.

"We worked our whole lifetimes to earn what Kevin does in one ballgame," Kevin's mother, Carolyn, said.

Family has always been important to Kevin. He was taught that there is a right way and a wrong way to go about your business.

When Kevin was 11 years old, his mother was diagnosed with a brain tumor. Kevin dropped out of football to help her with the physical therapy sessions.

Years later he proposed to his high school sweetheart on bended knee on Christmas Eve with the family videotaping the event. Rival batters may find it surprising, but Kevin does have a heart of gold when it comes to family and friends.

"Those are the people that you take care of first and never forget," he said.

Even though Kevin loved sports growing up, especially baseball and football, he never thought he could earn a living playing them. He thought he would work for Engelhard, just like so many in his family had and still do. He figured that after college he would live where he grew up—in tiny McIntyre.

On the north side of town, just past the small downtown consisting of a pharmacy, a bait and tackle shop and a gas station, lies a ballfield overgrown with weeds. This is where Kevin played softball during the summers for the Engelhard team. That's how certain he was that he would eventually work for the company.

"I have no doubt that Kevin could have fit right in with this community, if it hadn't been for baseball," said Jeff Dixon of Engelhard. "He doesn't live here anymore, but he still visits. We will always consider him one of our own."

Just north of town there are vast piles of white kaolin. Atop the highest mound, a bulldozer works away. The small plant off to the right is the machine shop. That's where Kevin's father worked for several decades.

It's a 15-minute ride from this mine site, the Gibraltar Site, to where Kevin's family used to live.

It seems that everybody has a favorite story about Kevin, and Dixon is no different.

"It was in the Kaolin Bowl, which is the biggest football game around here," he said. "Kevin was 12, maybe 13. On defense, he played safety and outside linebacker. Teams that ran to his side of the field never picked up that much yardage.

"But one year in the Kaolin Bowl, I remember they were gaining some real estate. I remember Kevin getting pretty agitated about it. He didn't

Kevin, who majored in chemical engineering at Georgia Tech, had to be talked into trying out for the baseball team. (Georgia Tech)

like it much, and, you know something? He quickly put an end to it."

Kevin's family home is on Route 57 in between the towns of Gordon and McIntyre. It is a small brick house overshadowed by two tall oak trees in the yard. According to the map, the house is in the center of this world, almost the same distance from the mine and the Little League Field, from the high school and railroad tracks.

Kaolin is the correct term for what is harvested from the ground. To those who do the work, they will always be chalk miners. That's what they were called 75 years ago when the first quarries and plants were set up. One gets the feeling no matter how far Kevin goes from home, that's what he'll always consider himself as well.

CHAPTER TWO

The Blade

Though it may sound amazing, Kevin was almost overlooked coming out of high school. If it wasn't for a persistent college coach and some good fortune, Kevin would almost certainly have ended up working in the town where he grew up.

Because Wilkinson County is so rural, and Kevin was never considered the best athlete among his peers, no professional scouts came to rate him when he was in high school, where he played baseball, football and tennis.

After graduating from Wilkinson High, Kevin decided to become a chemical engineer and work for Engelhard. To reach his goal, he decided to attend Georgia Tech as a co-op student. After a semester at college, he would spend the next semester working for the hometown company. After graduation, he would have a full-time job with Engelhard.

That was the plan—until Kevin played in a local baseball tournament the summer before he began classes at Georgia Tech. Julian Morgan, a scout for the New York Mets, saw him at that tournament and liked Kevin's "live arm."

Morgan told Jim Morris, then the coach at Georgia Tech, about Kevin and urged him to get the hard-throwing right-hander on his team.

At first, Kevin wasn't that interested in trying out. He was eager to begin his schoolwork, and playing baseball didn't seem like it would lead to anything of consequence.

"Kevin loved the game," said Morris. "That was apparent to anybody who got to know him. But he was ready to move on with his life and he wasn't sure that baseball was really that big a part of it anymore. Kevin had made some decisions about his life and he wanted to move ahead with them."

If it had been anybody else but Julian Morgan vouching for Kevin's baseball ability, Morris admits that he probably would have let the matter slide.

"But Julian told me that he liked how Kevin approached the game," Morris remembered. "He said that Kevin was very, very crude when it came to baseball. But that he a really good arm and a ball that sank. That got my attention."

So Morris continued to talk things over with Kevin.

"I was skeptical," Kevin said. "I mean, I was ready to go to school, become an engineer and now, out of the blue, people were telling me I had a future in baseball when I never thought I did."

What complicated matters was that if Kevin continued with the co-op program he would soon be ineligible to play college sports.

"I had to talk him into trying out for the team," Morris said. "At the time, it was a bit of a leap of faith on Kevin's part. I couldn't offer him a scholarship in the beginning. So he was giving up something sure for a chance to play baseball."

Even after he had convinced Kevin to come out for the team, Morris realized that his freshman right-hander wasn't like most of his players.

First, Kevin "was very, very intelligent," Morris said. "You can't simply tell him to do something. He wants to know why."

In three years at Georgia Tech, Kevin set records for victories (28) and strikeouts (249). (Georgia Tech)

Kevin also arrived on the team with a down-to-earth view of things and his role in them.

"So many kids arrive in college and they have been stars elsewhere. They are used to being superstars," Morris said. "But Kevin had never expected to play college ball, so he had no expectations at all. A lot of kids coming today have this attitude that are they are best in everything. Some of them make the mistake of not working hard at the next level. Kevin was never like that. He never thought he was 'the man,' so to speak, and everybody had to follow him. He just went out and worked hard. In a way that was pretty refreshing."

Kevin was a skinny kid when he joined the Yellow Jackets, and he was quickly nicknamed "Blade."

He soon earned a place in the Georgia Tech lineup and was a freshman All-American. However, neither Kevin nor Morris thought he had a big future in the major leagues until his junior year. Then, at a game against the University of Maryland Terrapins, Morris noticed something. Kevin was really throwing hard.

"Until that point, Kevin had thrown in the mid-80s," Morris remembered. "In fact, that's about where he had thrown in his previous start. But on this day I remember the ball really popping in the catcher's glove and for kicks I asked one of the scouts who was there to time him on his radar gun.

"The reading came back that Kevin was throwing 92, 93 mph," Morris recalled. "I've never had a pitcher gain that much velocity in between starts. Nobody. I mean that it was pretty unusual no matter what level of baseball you're at. But in a way, maybe that sums up Kevin. Like I said, he is very intelligent and, as an athlete, it's possible for him to make these big leaps in ability and confidence. If you look at his career, it's happened time and time again."

With pitches like that, Kevin and his coach soon realized, he was ready for a future in professional ball. Abandoning his goal of following his father into a career at Engelhard, Kevin headed for a career in the pros after three years of pitching for Georgia Tech. He left behind a school-record 28 victories and 249 strikeouts.

CHAPTER THREE

Deep in the Heart of Texas

Kevin was the fourth overall pick in the free-agent draft that June. The Texas Rangers snapped him up. They were a team on the rise, eager to add more pitching. For a long time, it appeared that Kevin would help lead them to their first World Series.

In those days, he was a young man in a hurry. After getting drafted, he made just three appearances in rookie ball and then was promoted to Double-A ball in Tulsa, Oklahoma, for three more games before getting called up to the parent club in late August. In less than four months, Kevin had gone from college ball to the major leagues.

Once he got to the top level, it took Kevin a long time to learn how to win start after start. Even though he showed such promise, making the majors in his first season, as the 1987 season unfolded he returned to the minors and spent that entire season there, losing 11 consecutive decisions. For much of that season, the majors seemed a long way away.

Perhaps part of the problem was the Rangers' coaches and managers. Kevin is the kind of guy who is used to doing things his own way and, as Jim Morris found out at Georgia Tech, this right-hander wants his questions answered.

"Kevin has always been a bit high strung," Morris said. "He expects to do well and he puts pressure on himself to do well. Sometimes that can lead to misunderstandings."

At Texas, the Rangers liked Kevin's collection of pitches. He had a lively fastball, a good sinkerball and soon added a deceptive changeup.

"He doesn't throw one straight pitch," said Bobby Valentine, then the Rangers' manager. "The changeup is bad news for hitters."

Such praise wasn't enough to keep Kevin, Valentine and Rangers pitching coach Tom House on the same page. After his disastrous season in 1987, where he went 1-11 in the minors, Kevin had formed some strong opinions about the best way to get hitters out. When he was called up to the majors for good, late in the 1988 season after winning 12 games at Tulsa, he wasn't especially open to more suggestions from Valentine and House.

"I overdosed on being perfect mechanically," Kevin said. "I decided to get back into the frame of mind that I had in college. Battle. Go to war and forget about everything else. As soon as I hit that mode, everything was all right."

While everything was all right on the mound, things never did really settle down between Kevin and the Rangers' coaching staff.

House, who was pitching coach for the first seven of Kevin's nine years in the Rangers' organization, once said that Kevin "is an Orel Hershiser with a 160 IQ. He's a (tall, skinny guy) with an overprocessing coconut."

In other words, Kevin thought a bit too much on the mound for the Rangers' taste.

"He's very, very bright, very talented, and rather volatile," House said. "We butted heads on occasion. But I think what happens with all young kids, you have a tendency to impose your mindset on them, rather than let the kid be a kid.

"He's a different personality, a strong personality. Probably the best thing would have been to let him go, just let him be himself."

Kevin pitched for the Baltimore Orioles in 1995, after leaving the Texas Rangers. (AP/Wide World Photos)

At the time, the Rangers didn't do that. They continued to work with Kevin on his mechanics. They also cautioned him to curb his temper and to try not to put too much pressure on himself. It seemed everybody had a suggestion for him—a way he could improve.

Kevin's time in Texas was like a roller coaster — almost as many dizzying downs as ups. In 1990, he went 12-10, the first time he reached double figures in victories in the majors. The next season he fell to 9-12. In 1992, he posted a league-leading 21 victories and 15 the next, but fell to 7-9 with a 4.82 ERA in 1994, his last year in Texas.

Observers maintain that part of the problem was the ongoing friction between Kevin and Valentine, who was the Rangers' manager until 1992.

"When a guy makes 30 starts and wins only nine with his stuff, it's hard to figure out why," Valentine said in 1991.

*Kevin defends the parking lot against batting practice
balls at the Marlins' spring training facility in 1996.
(AP/Wide World Photos)*

It also didn't help Kevin's standing within the Rangers' organization that he was the team's player representative during the baseball strike in 1994. When baseball came back the following season, Kevin got off to a 1-4 start and was getting booed in his home ballpark.

"I think if we would have said, 'Kevin, do it your way,' it would worked out better," ex-Rangers general manager Tom Grieve once told the (Fort Lauderdale) *Sun-Sentinel.* "Because he's going to do it his way. Trying to get him to be less intense or change his demeanor on the mound doesn't work. He's not going to be (calm like) Greg Maddux or Tom Glavine. He's Kevin Brown."

Kevin left Texas after the 1994 season and signed as a free agent with Baltimore. He stayed only one year with the Orioles, going 10-9.

As the 1996 season began, Kevin found himself with the Florida Marlins, a recent expansion team.

He had been in the majors more than six years, with a record of 88-73. Within baseball circles, he was regarded as a good, but not great, pitcher.

Still, Phil Regan, Baltimore's manager the year Kevin was there, insisted that the Marlins had found a possible diamond in the rough in Kevin.

"I think he's a little bit misunderstood, in that he's not a real outgoing person around the clubhouse. But who cares?" Regan told the *Port St. Lucie* (Florida) *News.* "As long as he takes the ball every fourth or fifth day and goes out and gives you six or seven innings. He always does that. He's always in shape, and he's got outstanding stuff and a rubber arm."

Morris, who had since moved from Georgia Tech to the University of Miami, said that Regan's scouting report pretty well summed up his former pitcher at the time.

"But what nobody realized was that Kevin had it in him to take it to another level," Morris said.

Indeed, soon Kevin would be recognized as one of the best pitchers in the game.

CHAPTER FOUR

No-Hitter and a World Championship

On June 12, 1997, Kevin served notice that he could be as dominating as any hurler around. Certainly, he had received some recognition before then. He won 17 games his first season with the Marlins and led the league with a 1.89 ERA—the first sub-2.00 ERA in a full season since Dwight Gooden's 1.53 in 1985. What he did that June day in San Francisco got everyone's attention. More importantly, it also set the tone for the Marlins' World Championship season

Kevin collides with Marlins first baseman Greg Colbrunn while fielding a fly ball. (AP/ Wide World Photos)

During his first seven starts in 1996, the Marlins scored only 11 runs for Kevin, leaving him with a 2-4 record despite his 2.26 ERA. (AP/Wide World Photos)

Kevin recorded a no-hitter, retiring 27 of the 28 San Francisco Giants who faced him that day. He barely missed a perfect game when his 1-2 pitch grazed Marvin Benard's leg with two outs in the eighth inning.

"The ball was moving all over the place," Giants first baseman J.T. Snow said. "You think you're right on the pitch and it ends up being off the end of the bat."

In his near perfect performance, Kevin retired 17 batters on ground balls, seven on strikeouts. Only three balls were hit in the air.

"It was Brownie's day, he was totally dominant," said Marlins manager Jim Leyland. "I didn't have anything to do with it. Anybody can spell 'Brown.' I put him in the ninth spot (in the batting order) and put No. 1 (his position) by his name. My mom can do that."

Kevin pitched a no-hitter for the Marlins on June 12, 1997. (AP/Wide World Photos)

Giants manager Dusty Baker added, "You need no-hitters in baseball sometimes. I remember as a kid, I used to beg my dad to take me to see Sandy Koufax pitch because he might throw a no-hitter. Today there are only a handful of pitchers you feel that way about."

After the game, Marlins equipment manager Mike Wallace shipped Kevin's cap and game ball to the Hall of Fame in Cooperstown, N.Y.

"I was real happy with the way turned out," Kevin said. "I've never pitched a game like this, not even in Little League.

"I've never really considered myself to be a candidate for a no-hitter. I'm more of a contact pitcher. I'm not the type of guy who can go out there and punch out 12 to 15 guys. So I've always been under the mindset that if a no-hitter happens, great. But I'm not really expecting it because I give up so many ground balls. It's kind of hard to have a game filled

In 1997, Kevin helped lead the Marlins to their first World Championship. (AP/Wide World Photos)

with ground balls and not have one find its way through."

As the Marlins transformed themselves into one of the best teams in the National League, they turned to Kevin more and more.

A month after his no-hitter in San Francisco, he shut down the Los Angeles Dodgers on one hit.

"He was a buzz saw," said Dodgers leadoff hitter Brett Butler. "He just wore us out."

In the playoffs, Kevin got even better. He held the Giants to one run over seven innings in the Division Series and then beat Maddux, the Braves' staff ace, twice in the League Championship Series. Still weak from a stomach virus, he struggled in the World Series, but in the end it didn't matter. He had led the Marlins that far and they weren't about to him down. The Marlins defeated the Cleveland Indians in seven games to capture their first world championship. Kevin thought he had found a home in south Florida.

CHAPTER FIVE

Leader of the Pack

Other than the Atlanta Braves, which have always been so loaded with pitching so as not to need his services, the Marlins rank as one of the closest franchises geographically to central Georgia, where Kevin grew up.

He said he would have liked to stay with that organization. But if some championship teams become winners for years, the Marlins were a shooting star across the heavens. Almost as soon as the celebration of their first World Series triumph faded into the night, the team began to be dismantled.

Business concerns forced the Marlins to deal most of the top players before the 1998 season, including Kevin. He and several other top Marlins went to management, begging to keep the team together, and let them defend their title. It wasn't to be.

Shortly before Christmas, Kevin was traded to San Diego, nearly a five-hour plane ride from his home. Perhaps earlier in his career, such a move would have angered Kevin, but he was a veteran now.

He soon found he had a friend in pitching coach Dave Stewart, who was known for his intensity while with the Oakland Athletics and the Toronto Blue Jays. Stewart asked Kevin to help him teach and motivate the Padres' young staff—Joey Hamilton, Sterling Hitchcock and Andy Ashby. Kevin said he would be happy to.

The San Diego Padres acquired Kevin in a trade less than two months after the Marlins won the World Series. (AP/ Wide World Photos)

"You learn so much from a guy like him," Ashby said. "Kevin hates to lose. He's so into every game he's out there. His concentration is something. After watching how he went about his job, I saw how much more I had to improve on the mental side."

Long-time Padres leader Tony Gwynn added, "You can't have too many guys like (Kevin). When he's on the mound, we feel like nobody can beat us, and you can't put a price on that."

Even though Kevin still sometimes lets his temper run away from him (he tore down a clubhouse sign after a mediocre start once), Padres manager Bruce Bochy said he wouldn't want it any other way.

"His attitude is just right," Bochy said. "He's out there, he won't accept losing. He has a hard time accepting that he made one bad pitch. For other guys to see that, it makes a difference."

Kevin was one of the Padres' team leaders in 1998.
(AP/Wide World Photos)

Even though San Diego general manager Kevin Towers acknowledged that Kevin spent the 1998 season a long way from his family, it never impacted his pitching performance.

"It was tough on him," Towers said. "He was leaving a club that just won a world championship. He's going from the East Coast to the West Coast."

Night after night, Kevin was there for his teammates. He found that he didn't have to necessarily be on the mound to influence the game's outcome. At Stewart's urging, he talked with the other starting pitchers in between innings. He was routinely the first one out on the field to congratulate his teammates after a victory.

"If somebody can feed off that emotion, great," Kevin said. "Everybody has different things that push you. We have a lot of guys here who are intense. You can take that emotion with you to the bench."

Kevin takes outfield practice in San Diego the day before pitching against the Houston Astros in the 1998 National League Division Series. (AP/Wide World Photos)

With Kevin as one of their team leaders, the Padres first won the National League West and then upset the Houston Astros and the Atlanta Braves to reach the World Series.

Kevin was within four games of winning his second world championship in as many years. Waiting to disrupt those plans, however, were the New York Yankees.

The highly touted Yankees, who had set an American League record by winning 114 games in the regular season, as well as historic Yankee Stadium seemed to intimidate many of the Padres— but not Kevin. Even though his team was swept in four games, he pitched well and afterward many of the Yankees said they didn't want to face him again anytime soon.

*Kevin returned to the World Series with the Padres in
1998, but they were swept by the Yankees in four games.
(AP/Wide World Photos)*

CHAPTER SIX

The $100 Million Man

Timing is everything in sports, and after the 1998 season Kevin became a free agent with nearly everybody realizing that he had become one of the best clutch pitchers around.

At first, the four-time All-Star wanted to stay in San Diego. Even though the city remained a long way from home, he believed the team could soon return to the World Series.

"That's the bottom-line with me," he said. "I want to be on a team that has a chance to contend."

Kevin became baseball's first $100 million man when the Los Angeles Dodgers signed him to a seven-year, $105 million contract in December, 1998. (AP/Wide World Photos)

When the Padres lost Ken Caminiti and Steve Finley to free agency, however, Kevin began to look elsewhere. The Rockies, the Diamondbacks, the Cardinals, the Rangers, the Orioles and the Dodgers were among the teams interested.

"I think Kevin is looking at a big payday," said Morris, his old college coach. "A big payday."

Little did Morris or the rest of the baseball world realize how big that payday would eventually be. The Dodgers eventually made Kevin baseball's first $100 million man. He was the first in baseball to reach that financial plateau.

Until that point, the only other athletes to sign such a huge contract were in the National Basketball Association—Kevin Garnett, Shaquille O'Neal, Alonzo Mourning, Shawn Kemp and Juwan Howard.

In baseball's pitcher-hungry world, Kevin was deemed worthy of such a big salary. After all, over

Kevin believes the 1999 Los Angeles Dodgers will be "a great team." (AP/Wide World Photos)

the previous two seasons, he had led the Florida Marlins and then the San Diego Padres to the World Series. In the Division Series, he had a 0.85 ERA. In the League Championship Series, it was barely above 1.00.

Despite throwing nearly 2,200 innings heading into the 1999 season, he had never been on the disabled list. The only other pitcher who could make a similar claim was Maddux.

Although Dodgers general manager Kevin Malone said he was bothered by paying that much money, he added that if he didn't "sign Kevin Brown, I guarantee you one or two or three other clubs are going to pay just as much or more. This is a special player. He makes everyone else better. I look at it as we've signed the best pitcher in baseball."

While admittedly stunned by the size of the Dodger contract—$105 million over seven years— Kevin said that the major factors again were how

Kevin has two sons: Ridge, at left (shown here with Padres batboy Joe Tarantino, manager Bruce Bochy's son, Brett, and Coach Rob Picciolo's son, Dusty) and Grayson. (AP/Wide World Photos)

well the team could compete and how it would impact his family.

"We're going to have a great team," he said. "I'm going be a guy who will take the ball every fourth or fifth day and hopefully give the team a chance to win every time out."

To shorten the travel time between Los Angeles and his home in Georgia, the Dodgers will let Kevin and his family use a private jet 12 times a season. That shortens the trip by 2 1/2 hours.

"We were looking at teams closer to home because my wife has always had to bear the largest part of the burden of raising the kids during the season," Kevin told the *Los Angeles Times*. "Being with the Padres last season, it was difficult being away from them. But the Dodgers made it easier on my wife and kids to come out there more often, a lot easier than I thought it could be."

Kevin has two sons, Ridge and Grayson. They were regulars in the Marlins' and Padres' clubhouses. Friends expect that the routine won't change now that Kevin has moved to the Dodgers.

"Family is the most important thing," Brown said. "That's the way it's always been with me. That's the way it has to be."

Opposite page: Kevin is looking for the Dodgers to have a big year in 1999. (AP/Wide World Photos)

After nine seasons in the American League, Kevin now bats for himself during games. (AP/Wide World Photos)

Kevin Brown Quick Facts

Full Name: James Kevin Brown
Team: Los Angeles Dodgers
Hometown: McIntyre, Georgia
Position: Pitcher
Jersey Number: 27
Bats: Right
Throws: Right
Height: 6-4
Weight: 195 pounds
Birthdate: March 14, 1965

1998 Highlight: Led the San Diego Padres to the National League pennant and the World Series for the first time since 1984.

Stats Spotlight: In 1998, he finished among the top three National League pitchers in earned-run average, shutouts and strikeouts.

Little-Known Fact: Majored in chemical engineering at Georgia Tech.

Kevin Brown's Professional Career

Year	Club	W-L	ERA	G	GS	CG	SHO	SV	IP	H	R	ER	BB	SO
1986	Texas	1-0	3.60	1	1	0	0	0	5	6	2	2	0	4
1988	Texas	1-1	4.24	4	4	1	0	0	23.1	33	15	11	8	12
1989	Texas	12-9	3.35	28	28	7	0	0	191	167	81	71	70	104
1990	Texas	12-10	3.60	26	26	6	2	0	180	175	84	72	60	88
1991	Texas	9-12	4.40	33	33	0	0	0	210.2	233	116	103	90	96
1992	Texas	21*-11	3.32	35	35	11	1	0	265.2	262*	117	98	76	173
1993	Texas	15-12	3.59	34	34	12	3	0	233	228	105	93	74	142
1994	Texas	7-9	4.82	26	25*	3	0	0	170	218*	109	91	50	123
1995	Baltimore	10-9	3.60	26	26	3	1	0	172.1	155	73	69	48	117
1996	Florida	17-11	1.89*	32	32	5	3*	0	233	187	60	49	33	159
1997	Florida	16-8	2.69	33	33	6	2	0	237.1	214	77	71	66	205
1998	San Diego	18-7	2.38	36	35*	7	3	0	257	225	77	68	49	257

M.L. Totals		139-99	3.30	314	312	61	15	0	2178.1	2103	916	798	624	1480

* Indicates League Leader

1998 NL ERA Leaders

Greg Maddux	2.22
Kevin Brown	**2.38**
Al Leiter	2.47
Tom Glavine	2.47
Omar Daal	2.88
John Smoltz	2.90
Dustin Hermanson	3.13
Pete Harnisch	3.14
Curt Schilling	3.25
Francisco Cordova	3.31

In 1998, Kevin was chosen as a member of the National League's All-Star pitching staff. (AP/Wide World Photos)

1998 NL Cy Young Award Voting

Tom Glavine	94
Trevor Hoffman	88
Kevin Brown	**76**
John Smoltz	10
Greg Maddux	10
Al Leiter	3
Randy Johnson	2

1998 NL W-L Percentage Leaders

John Smoltz	17-3	.850
Tom Glavine	20-6	.769
Al Leiter	17-6	.739
Kevin Brown	**18-7**	**.720**
Shane Reynolds	19-8	.704
Mark Gardner	13-6	.684
Kerry Wood	13-6	.684
Kevin Millwood	17-8	.680
Kevin Tapani	19-9	.679
Greg Maddux	18-9	.667

1998 NL Opposition BA Leaders

Kerry Wood	.196
Al Leiter	.216
Greg Maddux	.220
Pete Harnisch	.228
John Smoltz	.231
Dustin Hermanson	.234
Kevin Brown	**.235**
Curt Schilling	.236
Tom Glavine	.238
Chan Ho Park	.244

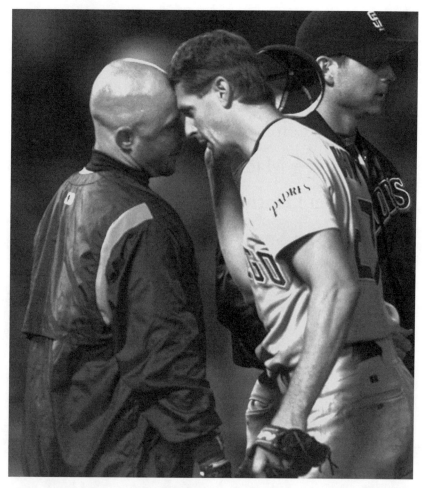

Teammate Jim Leyritz, left, congratulates Kevin after the Padres' victory over the Atlanta Braves in Game 2 of the National League Championship Series. (AP/Wide World Photos)

1998 NL Games Started Leaders

Kevin Brown	**35**
Daryl Kile	35
Shane Reynolds	35
Curt Schilling	35
10 Pitchers Tied	34

1998 NL Complete Games Leaders

Curt Schilling	15
Greg Maddux	9
Livan Hernandez	9
Kevin Brown	**7**
Carlos Perez	7

1998 NL Wins Leaders

Tom Glavine	20
Kevin Tapani	19
Shane Reynolds	19
Greg Maddux	18
Kevin Brown	**18**

1998 NL Shutout Leaders

Greg Maddux	5
Randy Johnson	4
Tom Glavine	3
Kevin Brown	**3**
9 Pitchers Tied	2

1998 Batters Faced Leaders

Curt Schilling	1089
Livan Hernandez	1040
Kevin Brown	**1032**
Darryl Kile	1020
Carlos Perez	1009

1998 Innings Pitched Leaders

Curt Schilling	268.2
Kevin Brown	**257.0**
Greg Maddux	251.0
Carlos Perez	241.0
Livan Hernandez	234.1

Kevin struck out 257 batters in 1998. (AP/Wide World Photos)

1998 Strikeout Leaders

Curt Schilling	300
Kevin Brown	**257**
Kerry Wood	233
Shane Reynolds	209
Greg Maddux	204

Active CG Frequency Leaders

Curt Schilling	.26
Roger Clemens	.25
Dave Stieb	.25
Jack McDowell	.23
Greg Maddux	.22
Bret Saberhagen	.22
Kevin Brown	**.20**
Randy Johnson	.20

Active Career GDPs
Induced Leaders

Greg Maddux	247
Kevin Brown	**235**
Chuck Finley	232
Orel Hershiser	231
Tom Glavine	227
Scott Erickson	224
Mike Morgan	216
Bill Swift	206
Mark Langston	192
Jim Abbott	190

Active Career HR/9 IP Leaders

Greg Maddux	.45
John Franco	.49
Kevin Brown	**.50**
Roger Clemens	.59
Dwight Gooden	.59
Tom Glavine	.59
Kevin Appier	.62
Al Leiter	.62
Mike Maddux	.64
Bill Swift	.65

Kevin Brown's
Career Highlights

1999:

- Signed by the Los Angeles Dodgers in December of 1998, to a seven-year contract.

- Begins the '99 season with a career record of 139-99 and a 3.30 earned-run average.

- Career statistics show him with 1,480 strikeouts, while allowing just 624 walks.

1998:

- Traded from Florida to San Diego on December 15, 1997, he led the Padres to the National League pennant.

- Finished the season with an 18-7 record and a 2.38 ERA in 36 games.

- Totaled 257 strikeouts in his 257 innings, allowing only 49 walks all season long.

- Tied for first in National League starts, second in ERA and strikeouts, tied for third with three shutouts, tied for fourth in wins, fourth in strikeouts per nine innings with 9.0, and fifth in winning percentage (.720).

- Surrendered three earned runs or less in 31 of his 35 starts, worked 7.0 innings or more in 16 of his last 19 starts, and went at least 8.0 innings in 15 of his outings.

- Led the National League with an 11-game winning streak, and propelled the Padres to a 22-13 record in his 35 starts.

- Fanned a career-high 11 batters on four different occasions and recorded nine of his 19 career double-digit Ks in 1998.

- Seventy-five percent of the balls hit into play off Brown remained on the ground.

- A strong finisher, he went 15-4 with a 2.32 ERA in his final 26 games.

- During his seven losses in 1998, he posted a 3.24 ERA, yet his offense supplied him with just 13 total runs.

- As the Padres' stopper, Brown enabled San Diego to go 9-2 when he took the mound following a loss.

1997:

- Compiled a 16-8 record and a 2.69 ERA in 33 starts for the World Champion Florida Marlins.

- Threw a no-hitter on June 10 against San Francisco, striking out seven, and allowing just one baserunner, a hit batsman.

- Set career-high with 205 strikeouts.

- Tied Greg Maddux with 81.8 percent Quality Start percentage.

- Led Major Leagues by allowing just .136 average in close-and-late situations.

1996:

- Runner-up in National League Cy Young voting in 1996, posting 17-11 record, but leading N.L. with 1.89 ERA.
- Marlins scored just 11 runs in his 11 losses.
- Allowed lowest slugging percentage in the league.
- Named to National League All-Star Team.
- Struck out 1,000th career hitter on September 12.
- Signed with Marlins as free agent on December 22, 1995.

1995:

- As a member of the Baltimore Orioles, he finished seventh in the American League in ERA (3.60) and opponents batting average against (.241).

- Allowed only 0.52 home runs per 9.0 innings pitched, the second-best ratio in the league behind Randy Johnson's 0.50.

- As a fielder, he led the AL with 40 putouts and 84 total chances.

- Suffered a dislocated right index finger on June 22 vs. Boston, placing him on disabled list for 26 days.

- With a victory on September 17th, he improved his career record vs. the Yankees to 12-3.

- Reached double figures in wins (10) for the fifth time in the last seven years.

1994:

- Started the season for the Texas Rangers with a four-game losing streak.

- Worked at least seven innings in 16 of his 25 starts.

- Made his first Major League relief appearance on May 10 vs. California after 169 career starts.
- Tied his career high with 10 strikeouts on July 5 vs. Cleveland. He had fanned 10 batters in a game only twice before.

1993:

- As a Texas Ranger, he ranked second in the majors with 12 complete games and tied for second in the American League with three shutouts.
- Tossed 200+ innings for the third straight year and ranked 10th in the AL in innings pitched.
- Allowed only 14 home runs, the second-best ratio among AL starters.
- Fanned a career-high 10 batters twice during the season.
- Shared AL Player of the Week honors for May 3-9 with Oakland's Mark McGwire.

1992:

- Tied Toronto's Jack Morris for AL lead in wins with 21.

- Joined Ferguson Jenkins as the Rangers' only 20-game winners.

- Led the AL with 265.2 IP and ranked among league leaders in complete games (11), starts (35), winning percentage (.656), strikeouts (173) and ERA (3.32).

- Was first-ever Rangers pitcher to start an All-Star Game and was winning hurler in the game at San Diego.

1991:

- Led the Rangers in starts (33) and innings pitched (210.2).

1990:

- Became the first Ranger ever to win his first five starts in a season.
- Tied for club lead in shutouts (2) and tied for third in wins (12).
- Tied for sixth in AL in shutouts and tied for eighth with six complete games.

1989:

- Voted Texas Rangers' Rookie of the Year in 1989.
- Led Major League rookies with seven complete games and a 3.35 ERA.
- Tied Rangers' rookie record with 12 wins.
- Placed fifth in AL Rookie of the Year voting and was named to *Baseball Digest's* Major League All-Rookie Team.

1988:

- Began the season at AA Tulsa.

- Promoted to Texas on September 12 and two days later hurled a six-hit complete game win at Oakland in his first start, taking a shutout into the ninth inning.

1986:

- Promoted to Rangers on September 5 after only two minor league starts. Defeated Oakland on September 30 as a starter in his only appearance. Became only the third pitcher to win first pro game at Major League level.

Derek Jeter:
The Yankee Kid

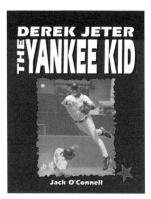

Author: Jack O'Connell
ISBN: 1-58261-043-6

In 1996 Derek burst onto the scene as one of the most promising young shortstops to hit the big leagues in a long time. His hitting prowess and ability to turn the double play have definitely fulfilled the early predictions of greatness.

A native of Kalamazoo, MI, Jeter has remained well grounded. He patiently signs autographs and takes time to talk to the young fans who will be eager to read more about him in this book.

Bernie Williams:
Quiet Superstar

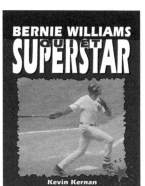

Author: Kevin Kernan
ISBN: 1-58261-044-4

Bernie Williams, a guitar-strumming native of Puerto Rico, is not only popular with his teammates, but is considered by top team officials to be the heir to DiMaggio and Mantle fame.

He draws frequent comparisons to Roberto Clemente, perhaps the greatest player ever from Puerto Rico. Like Clemente, Williams is humble, unassuming, and carries himself with quiet dignity. Also like Clemente, he plays with rare determination and a special elegance. He's married, and serves as a role model not only for his three children, but for his young fans here and in Puerto Rico.

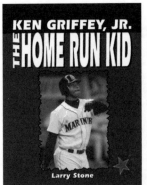

Ken Griffey, Jr.: The Home Run Kid

Author: Larry Stone
ISBN: 1-58261-041-x

Capable of hitting majestic home runs, making breathtaking catches, and speeding around the bases to beat the tag by a split second, Ken Griffey, Jr. is baseball's Michael Jordan. Amazingly, Ken reached the Major Leagues at age 19, made his first All-Star team at 20, and produced his first 100 RBI season at 21.

The son of Ken Griffey, Sr., Ken is part of the only father-son combination to play in the same outfield together in the same game, and, like Barry Bonds, he's a famous son who turned out to be a better player than his father.

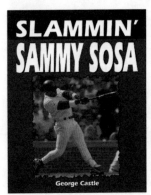

Sammy Sosa: Slammin' Sammy

Author: George Castle
ISBN: 1-58261-029-0

1998 was a break-out year for Sammy as he amassed 66 home runs, led the Chicago Cubs into the playoffs and finished the year with baseball's ultimate individual honor, MVP.

When the national spotlight was shone on Sammy during his home run chase with Mark McGwire, America got to see what a special person he is. His infectious good humor and kind heart have made him a role model across the country.

Omar Vizquel: The Man with the Golden Glove

Author: Dennis Manoloff
ISBN: 1-58261-045-2

Omar has a career fielding percentage of .982 which is the highest career fielding percentage for any shortstop with at least 1,000 games played.

Omar is a long way from his hometown of Caracas, Venezuela, but his talents as a shortstop put him at an even greater distance from his peers while he is on the field.

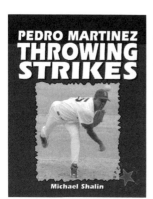

Pedro Martinez: Throwing Strikes

Author: Mike Shalin
ISBN: 1-58261-047-9

The 1997 National League Cy Young Award winner is always teased because of his boyish looks. He's sometimes mistaken for the batboy, but his curve ball and slider leave little doubt that he's one of the premier pitchers in the American League.

It is fitting that Martinez is pitching in Boston, where the passion for baseball runs as high as it does in his native Dominican Republic.

Nomar Garciaparra: High 5!

Author: Mike Shalin
ISBN: 1-58261-053-3

An All-American at Georgia Tech, a star on the 1992 U.S. Olympic Team, the twelfth overall pick in the 1994 draft, and the 1997 American League Rookie of the Year, Garciaparra has exemplified excellence on every level.

At shortstop, he'll glide deep into the hole, stab a sharply hit grounder, then throw out an opponent on the run. At the plate, he'll uncoil his body and deliver a clutch double or game-winning homer. Nomar is one of the game's most complete players.

Juan Gonzalez: Juan Gone!

Author: Evan Grant
ISBN: 1-58261-048-7

One of the most prodigious and feared sluggers in the major leagues, Gonzalez was a two-time home run king by the time he was 24 years old.

After having something of a personal crisis in 1996, the Puerto Rican redirected his priorities and now says baseball is the third most important thing in his life after God and family.

Mo Vaughn:
Angel on a Mission

Author: Mike Shalin
ISBN: 1-58261-046-0

Growing up in Connecticut, this Angels slugger learned the difference between right and wrong and the value of honesty and integrity from his parents early on, lessons that have stayed with him his whole life.

This former American League MVP was so active in Boston charities and youth programs that he quickly became one of the most popular players ever to don the Red Sox uniform.

Mo will be a welcome addition to the Angels line-up and the Anaheim community.

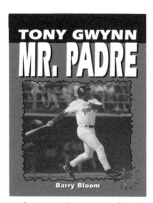

Tony Gwynn:
Mr. Padre

Author: Barry Bloom
ISBN: 1-58261-049-5

Tony is regarded as one of the greatest hitters of all-time. He is one of only three hitters in baseball history to win eight batting titles (the others: Ty Cobb and Honus Wagner).

In 1995 he won the Branch Rickey Award for Community Service by a major leaguer. He is unfailingly humble and always accessible, and he holds the game in deep respect. A throwback to an earlier era, Gwynn makes hitting look effortless, but no one works harder at his craft.

Sandy and Roberto Alomar: Baseball Brothers

Author: Barry Bloom
ISBN: 1-58261-054-1

Sandy and Roberto Alomar are not just famous baseball brothers they are also famous baseball sons. Sandy Alomar, Sr. played in the major leagues fourteen seasons and later went into management. His two baseball sons have made names for themselves and have appeared in multiple All-Star games.

With Roberto joining Sandy in Cleveland, the Indians look to be a front-running contender in the American League Central.

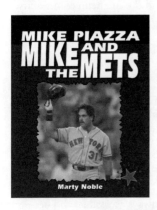

Mike Piazza: Mike and the Mets

Author: Marty Noble
ISBN: 1-58261-051-7

A total of 1,389 players were selected ahead of Mike Piazza in the 1988 draft, who wasn't picked until the 62nd round, and then only because Tommy Lasorda urged the Dodgers to take him as a favor to his friend Vince Piazza, Mike's father.

Named in the same breath with great catchers of another era like Bench, Dickey and Berra, Mike has proved the validity of his father's constant reminder "If you work hard, dreams do come true."

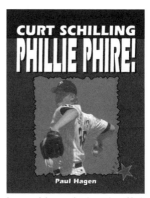

Curt Schilling: Phillie Phire!
Author: Paul Hagen
ISBN: 1-58261-055-x

Born in Anchorage, Alaska, Schilling has found a warm reception from the Philadelphia Phillies faithful. He has amassed 300+ strikeouts in the past two seasons and even holds the National League record for most strikeouts by a right handed pitcher at 319.

This book tells of the difficulties Curt faced being traded several times as a young player, and how he has been able to deal with off-the-field problems.

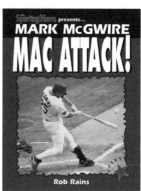

Mark McGwire: Mac Attack!
Author: Rob Rains
ISBN: 1-58261-004-5

Mac Attack! describes how McGwire overcame poor eyesight and various injuries to become one of the most revered hitters in baseball today. He quickly has become a legendary figure in St. Louis, the home to baseball legends such as Stan Musial, Lou Brock, Bob Gibson, Red Schoendienst and Ozzie Smith. McGwire thought about being a police officer growing up, but he hit a home run in his first Little League at-bat and the rest is history.

Roger Clemens: Rocket Man!
Author: Kevin Kernan
ISBN: 1-58261-128-9

Alex Rodriguez: A-plus Shortstop
ISBN: 1-58261-104-1

SUPERSTAR SERIES

Collect Them All!

Baseball
SuperStar Series Titles

____ **Sandy and Roberto Alomar: Baseball Brothers**

____ **Kevin Brown: Kevin with a "K"**

____ **Roger Clemens: Rocket Man!**

____ **Juan Gonzalez: Juan Gone!**

____ **Mark Grace: Winning With Grace**

____ **Ken Griffey, Jr.: The Home Run Kid**

____ **Tony Gwynn: Mr. Padre**

____ **Derek Jeter: The Yankee Kid**

____ **Randy Johnson: Arizona Heat!**

____ **Pedro Martinez: Throwing Strikes**

____ **Mike Piazza: Mike and the Mets**

____ **Alex Rodriguez: A-plus Shortstop**

____ **Curt Schilling: Philly Phire!**

____ **Sammy Sosa: Slammin' Sammy**

____ **Mo Vaughn: Angel on a Mission**

____ **Omar Vizquel: The Man with a Golden Glove**

____ **Larry Walker: Colorado Hit Man!**

____ **Bernie Williams: Quiet Superstar**

____ **Mark McGwire: Mac Attack!**

Available by calling 877-424-BOOK